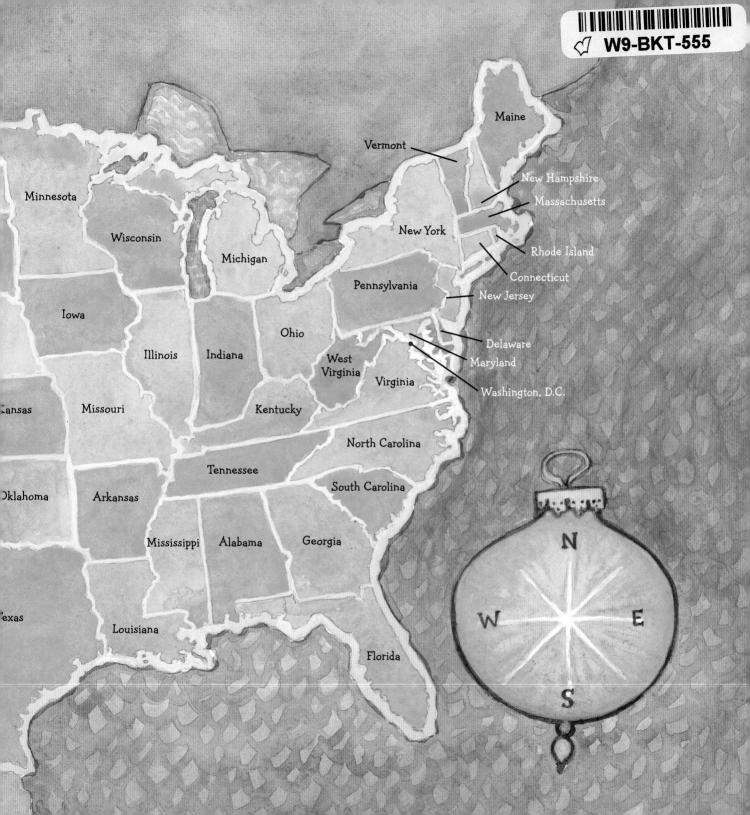

W9-BKT-555

Minnesota

Wisconsin

Michigan

Iowa

Illinois

Indiana

Ohio

Missouri

Kentucky

ansas

West
Virginia

Virginia

Oklahoma

Arkansas

Tennessee

North Carolina

South Carolina

Mississippi

Alabama

Georgia

exas

Louisiana

Florida

Vermont

Maine

New Hampshire

Massachusetts

New York

Pennsylvania

Rhode Island

Connecticut

New Jersey

Delaware

Maryland

Washington, D.C.

N

W   E

S

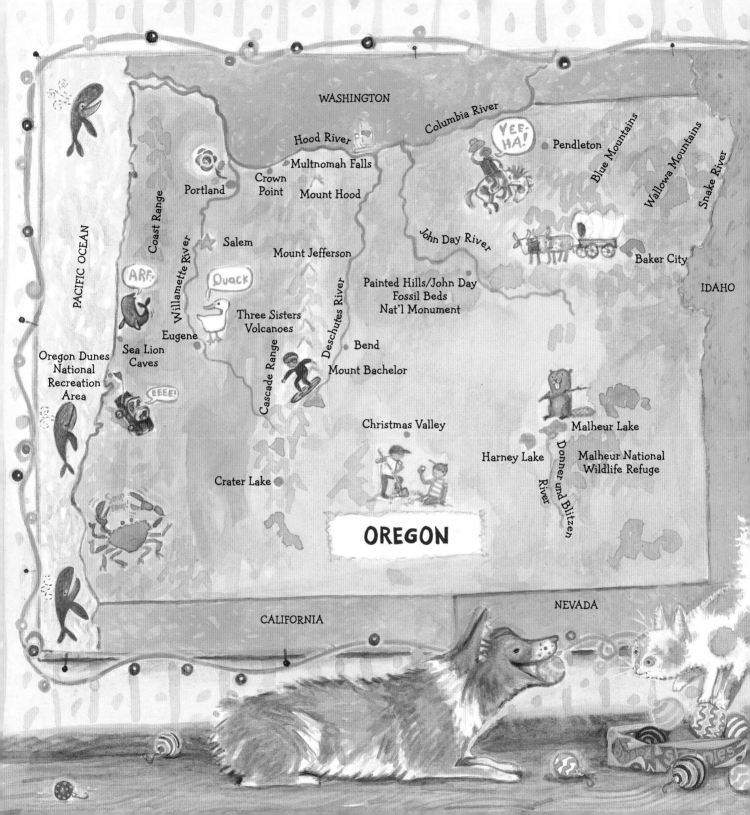

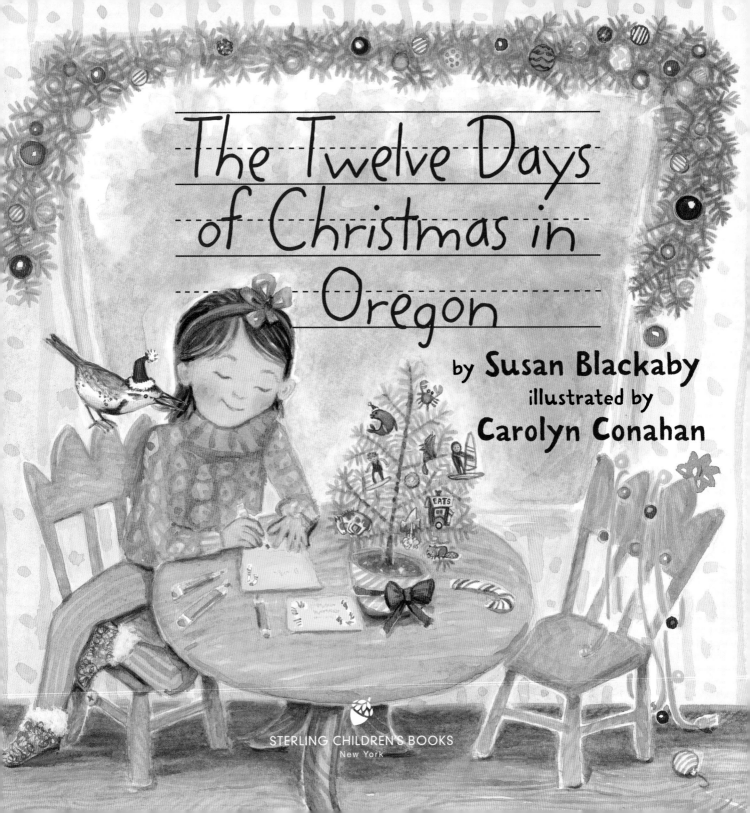

The Twelve Days of Christmas in Oregon

by Susan Blackaby

illustrated by
Carolyn Conahan

STERLING CHILDREN'S BOOKS
New York

Dear Damon,

Hooray! I'm so excited you're spending the holidays in Oregon. Just wait until you see your home away from home. Next time we'll make room for Brody and your sisters, too. This time, get ready for plenty of surprises!

We're going to show you all the sights from the rainforest to the desert to the mountains to the beach. You'll snowboard on a huge volcano, bike through the biggest city in the state, and dip your toes in the Pacific Ocean. You'll see forests and fields, rivers and critters, and get expert commentary from Mom.

We've mapped out a whirlwind tour, so as Grandpa says, "Hold on to your hat!" On second thought, make that LOTS of hats, plus a cap, a hood, and a helmet. You are "heading" (get it?) for all kinds of activities in all kinds of conditions, and we never let bad weather spoil the fun. Oh, and be sure to bring an extra-large duffel. You won't believe the gifts I've picked out for your twelve days of Christmas in Oregon!

Your Portland cousin,

Liz

P.S. Do Oregonians really have webbed feet? You'll find out!

Dear Mom and Dad,

Flying into Portland, you glide over forests and farms as you follow the river to the airport. Green on green on GREEN!

Liz and Aunt Deb met me at the airport exit gate, and then Grandpa pulled up towing a cottage on wheels! Liz had decorated the porch with twinkle lights and a Douglas-fir seedling in a pot. Grandpa says it's the state tree, and we'll have to plant it with room to grow—Douglas-fir trees get to be hundreds of feet tall. No kidding! The forest along the Historic Columbia River Highway is full of them, and they're ginormous.

Our first official stop was Vista House—an observatory on top of a giant bluff called Crown Point. It gives you a stupendous view of the Columbia River. While we were there, a bird perched on my treetop. Aunt Deb called him a western meadowlark, the state bird. I'm going to call him Bo because he looks just like a bright yellow bow on a present. Liz says he showed up with a special hello—when he sings it sounds like he's saying, "Oregon is a pretty little place!" Totally true!

So far, so ~~good~~ <u>fantastic</u>,
Damon

P.S. I thought it was raining at Crown Point, but Liz says that sprinkles don't count.

On the first day of Christmas, my cousin gave to me . . .

a meadowlark in a fir tree.

Dear Mom and Dad,

Last night we camped beside the Columbia River, just like the explorers Lewis and Clark—except they didn't have a nice dry trailer to sleep in. It was pouring! (Liz says it was just a little shower.)

The Columbia creates most of the border between Oregon and Washington, and the Columbia River Gorge is where it cuts a steep canyon through the mountains. These mountains are called the Cascade Range because of all the waterfalls that tumble over the steep slopes. We passed cascade after cascade before we stopped at Multnomah Falls, named for a powerful chief who ruled the tribes in this area in the 1700s.

Multnomah Falls is gigantic. Aunt Deb says it's one of the tallest year-round waterfalls in the United States. The water drops about 620 feet from top to bottom (taller than a 60-story building!) and is split into two parts, called steps. We hiked up to the footbridge that crosses over the lower step. From there you can get a noisy, misty view of both steps as the water crashes down the cliff!

Yours till the waterfalls,

Damon

On the second day of Christmas, my cousin gave to me . . .

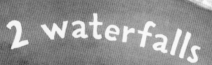

2 waterfalls

and a meadowlark in a fir tree.

Dear Mom and Dad,

Malheur National Wildlife Refuge includes a huge wetland that used to be part of an ancient lake. It is located in the high desert east of the Cascades. President Teddy Roosevelt set this area aside back in 1908 to give the millions of migrating birds on the Pacific Flyway a safe spot to rest. (Bo is taking it easy, too, even though he got here on the highway—haha.) There are also plenty of animals, including rabbits, mice, badgers, and weasels—a full menu for the raptors that spend the winter in the rimrock. We saw a Great Horned Owl that was almost as tall as Brody!

We camped near the Donner und Blitzen River (which comes from the German words for "thunder" and "lightning," just like the names of Santa's reindeer). It flows into Malheur Lake and joins Harney Lake to create a huge marsh, so it wasn't surprising to see a family of beavers working hard on a dam. Liz says their lodge is almost as cozy as ours. I'm glad. Between the coyotes, the birds of prey, and the cold, it's nice to be inside no matter what kind of critter you are!

Safe and sound and busy as—you guessed it!—an Oregon beaver!

Damon

P.S. Aunt Deb says <u>malheur</u> means "unhappiness" in French, but don't worry! I'm having a great time!

We should come here for vacation!

Donner und Blitzen River

On the third day of Christmas,
my cousin gave to me . . .

3 beavers

Merry Christmas

2 waterfalls,
and a meadowlark in a fir tree.

Dear Mom and Dad,

Today we collected thundereggs! They look like baseballs made of stone, but that's just the outside shell. Inside there can be bright gemstone crystals and layers of quartz and opal, but you can't tell what you'll find until you slice them open. Grandpa knows an old "rock hound" with a giant rock collection and a bunch of great tools, including a special saw. He sliced our thundereggs in half and polished them to bring out all the layers and colors. Amazing!

Native American legends say that the thunder spirits stole the "eggs" from thunderbirds' nests to lob at each other whenever they were angry—that's why these thundereggs are scattered all over the place. But Aunt Deb says they formed from bubbly lava during ancient volcanic eruptions. They come in all sizes, from as small as a grape to bigger than a beach ball—and all of them are full of surprises!

Near Christmas Valley we stopped to explore Fossil Lake—a dry lakebed where you can see 10,000-year-old remains of birds, fish, and mammals. Maybe Bo should change his tune. Oregon rocks!

Your rock hound,

Damon

On the fourth day of Christmas,
my cousin gave to me . . .

4 thundereggs

3 beavers, 2 waterfalls,
and a meadowlark in a fir tree.

Dear Mom and Dad,

Best day ever! I was afraid we wouldn't make it to Crater Lake because the road can be buried under 20 feet of snow in winter, but when cars can't get through, snowmobiles rule! We had a chilly picnic beside the deep blue lake—the deepest in the United States!

Aunt Deb says Crater Lake was formed when Mount Mazama erupted more than 7,000 years ago. I thought Crater Lake was great, but Liz prefers volcanoes that are still in one piece. She lives in the right place! The string of volcanic peaks in the Cascades is part of the Pacific Ring of Fire. Oregon's volcanoes haven't erupted in a long time, but experts say some of them may still be active. Mount Hood, Mount Jefferson, and the Three Sisters—North, South, and Middle—are all dormant ("sleeping") volcanoes over 10,000 feet high! They look quiet and peaceful right now, but I know from experience that sisters can blow their stacks at any time! (Just kidding! Haha!)

Lava and kisses from Bo and me,

Damon

Kerblooie!
Crater Lake
Mt Mazama

On the fifth day of Christmas,
my cousin gave to me . . .

5 snowy peaks

4 thundereggs, 3 beavers,
2 waterfalls, and a meadowlark in a fir tree.

Dear Mom and Dad,

Today started with snowboarding at Mount Bachelor. Not only is Mount Bachelor another volcano, it's also a ski resort where the United States Olympic ski and snowboarding teams often train!

I took a lesson and then went up the lift with Liz for my first official run. I fell down 57 times, but I didn't even care! Getting up gave me time to enjoy the deep, soft powder, blue sky, and amazing view. Liz stopped laughing at me after about the 29th time I face-planted. I may not be ready for boosting (that's when you catch air off a jump), but I'm learning!

After dinner Grandpa asked if we wanted some hot cocoa. Obviously! But it turned out we had to work for it. We took a moonlit snowshoe tour along a trail leading to the mouth of a cave called a lava tube. Liz and I put on headlamps and followed the guide into a network of underground tunnels that opened into big rocky rooms. We were careful not to disturb the Bo-sized bats dangling from the ceiling! Back outside we counted shooting stars. And we finally got our cocoa, too.

Love from the Bunny Slope!

Damon

On the sixth day of Christmas,
my cousin gave to me . . .

6 boarders boosting

5 snowy peaks, 4 thundereggs, 3 beavers,
2 waterfalls, and a meadowlark in a fir tree.

Dear Mom and Dad,

Today we stopped in the Painted Hills. They are part of the John Day Fossil Beds National Monument. Aunt Deb says this whole area of dry shrubland was once a tropical river valley. The plants that grew here and the fine sandy soil left behind from ancient floods have created fantastic layered hills in shades of red, gray, and gold.

We had lunch at the Oregon Trail Interpretive Center near Baker City. The exhibits and films show you just what it was like to head west in the 1800s. Liz and I sat in a prairie schooner just like the wagons the pioneers used for the dusty five-month trip.

From Baker City we wound up into the craggy peaks of the Wallowa Mountains, known as the Alps of Oregon. In the summer there are lots of hikers, anglers, and boaters helping themselves to all kinds of outdoor fun, but in the winter it is quieter— except for the night that we were there, that is. Gray wolves from the Snake River pack roam this part of Oregon. Aunt Deb says that the wolves here are in danger of becoming extinct and are protected and tracked by wildlife managers. We were so lucky to hear them, and they were just like Brody—they wouldn't pipe down!

Owooooooo!

Damon

P.S. If you are in the Polar Bear Club, like Grandpa, you can end the year with a swim in the icy lake! Brrr!

RAHR!

Who wants a swim?

Call me in July!

Moo!

On the seventh day of Christmas,
my cousin gave to me . . .

7 gray wolves howling

6 boarders boosting, 5 snowy peaks, 4 thundereggs,
3 beavers, 2 waterfalls, and a meadowlark in a fir tree.

Dear Mom and Dad,

On today's leg of the trip we followed the Oregon Trail to Pendleton, curving down the steep grade called Cabbage Hill. (It's named for a pioneer who grew cabbages nearby.) It is not an easy trip for kids and a bird in a car towing a trailer, so it must have been EXTRA tricky for oxen pulling a covered wagon. From the summit, you can see a frosty patchwork of wheat ranches stretching out to the Cascades halfway across the state.

Liz says the road leads to cowgirl country, but there are plenty of cowboys, too. Pendleton is known for its 10,000 years of tribal history; its wool blankets; and its roping, riding, and racing. The Pendleton Round-up, held every September, is a world-famous rodeo. We visited Tamástslikt, the tribal cultural center; toured the Pendleton Woolen Mills; and saw the Round-up exhibits at the Happy Canyon Hall of Fame. Then we took a bumpy horseback ride for our very own taste of the wild, wild west.

Yeehaw!

Damon

P.S. The Round-up motto is "Let 'Er Buck!" but clip-clopping was just fine with me!

Giddy-up!

munch, munch!

Oregon Trail

On the eighth day of Christmas,
my cousin gave to me . . .

8 broncos bucking

7 gray wolves howling, 6 boarders boosting,
5 snowy peaks, 4 thundereggs, 3 beavers,
2 waterfalls, and a meadowlark in a fir tree.

Dear Mom and Dad,

As much as I'd like to be a volcanologist, an Olympic skier, a wildlife expert, or a rodeo star when I grow up, I think I'll be a windsurfer instead. We are in Hood River, the windsurfing capital of the world, and the sailors are out on the water in their wetsuits, skimming across the Columbia River. They are 100% awesome.

The Columbia River Gorge is 80 miles long and over 4,000 feet deep in some places. Aunt Deb says the steep cliffs of the gorge create a natural wind tunnel—perfect conditions for one crazy sport!

When the wind is high, the water is wild. The sailors glide, loop, jump over the choppy whitecaps, and spin at top speed. It is totally fun to watch them race, but Liz has taken lessons in the summertime, and she says it is ten times more fun to be on the water than it is to be on shore. Count me in!

Cheers,

Damon

On the ninth day of Christmas, my cousin gave to me . . .

9 sailors surfing

8 broncos bucking, 7 gray wolves howling,
6 boarders boosting, 5 snowy peaks, 4 thundereggs,
3 beavers, 2 waterfalls, and a meadowlark in a fir tree.

Dear Mom and Dad,

We're in Portland, the Rose City! Portland is one of the greenest cities in the United States. You might think that's because of the trees, parks, and gardens (including thousands of rose bushes), but it's also because Portlanders try to take good care of the environment. Streetcars and trains zip all over the city, and there are 300 miles of bikeways for the pedal-pushing population.

In downtown's Pioneer Courthouse Square, there's a bronze statue of a man holding an umbrella, and he's the only person I saw using one! Real people just wear caps or hoods in the mists, drizzles, sprinkles, and showers.

Liz and Grandpa liked browsing the artists' booths at the Saturday Market near the river in Old Town. Bo and Deb and I liked visiting Packy, an elephant at the Oregon Zoo. And all of us liked eating! Portland is known for its fabulous food carts. We ate gooey grilled cheese, steamy bowls of Thai noodles, and veggie burgers made with BEETS!

We ended the day with a bike ride along the waterfront. Portland is the best place on two wheels!

Yours till the raindrops,

Damon

On the tenth day of Christmas, my cousin gave to me . . .

FOOD

Something Fishy

Veggie Tables

Sweeties

Patty's

CB

Cheez Bus

Jammin' Toast

Food-Shed

HOLA TACOS

10 Portland food carts

9 sailors surfing, **8** broncos bucking, **7** gray wolves howling,
6 boarders boosting, **5** snowy peaks, **4** thundereggs,
3 beavers, **2** waterfalls, and a meadowlark in a fir tree.

Dear Mom and Dad,

Today we traveled down the Willamette Valley, through 150 miles of vineyards, farms, and orchards tucked between the Cascades and the Coast Range. The valley is filled with sheep and cows and all sorts of crops—Christmas trees, fruits, nuts, vegetables, flowers, and even plain old grass! The Willamette Valley is the grass seed capital of the world! We stopped and bought honey, winter pears, and carrots at a farm market and passed the capitol building in Salem with its gold Oregon Pioneer statue on top before heading over the mountains to the Pacific Ocean.

The second we got to the coast I had my shoes OFF! Liz and I raced across the sand and splashed into the ice-cold surf. Bo mingled with the pelicans and gulls swooping over the beach.

When Grandpa mentioned the Sea Lion Caves, I expected a cramped, damp hole, but Oregon has one of the biggest sea caves in the world. The stony hall is as tall as a twelve-story building and is home to a herd of 200 sea lions barking like crazy. They are known for their little ears, huge size, strong smell, and nonstop talk!

Arf! Arf! Arf! from the edge of North America!

Damon

Pelican Catch!

On the eleventh day of Christmas,
my cousin gave to me . . .

11 sea lions barking

10 Portland food carts,
9 sailors surfing,
8 broncos bucking,
7 gray wolves howling,
6 boarders boosting,
5 snowy peaks,
4 thundereggs,
3 beavers, 2 waterfalls,
and a meadowlark in a fir tree.

Dear Mom and Dad,

As you know by now from my letters, Oregon is a great place to visit if you like mountains, and <u>today's</u> mountains were made of sand! This part of the Oregon coast has the biggest stretch of coastal sand dunes in North America. We went on a dune buggy tour that was like a roller-coaster ride except with goggles and helmets, a few more wild dips, sharper turns, and a cool view of the ocean!

The Dungeness crab is Oregon's official state crustacean, and you can see why when you meet the fleet! Aunt Deb has a friend who is a crabber. She took us out in her boat to catch our dinner. I liked helping Grandpa pull the crab pots out of the water. They look like wire hatboxes filled with wiggly legs and clampy claws.

We ended up having a huge crab feed on the beach, with a big bonfire and s'mores for dessert.

Speaking of s'mores, I need to spend s'more time exploring Oregon, but I promised Aunt Deb, Grandpa, and Liz that I'd bring all of you with me next time. You'll love it here.

Ho-ho-home tomorrow! You'd better pick me up in the pickup . . . Bo and I have lots to share!

Love,
Damon

On the twelfth day of Christmas, my cousin gave to me . . .

Inapinch

Krab-Bloaie

12 crabbers crabbing

Sandy Claws

11 sea lions barking, 10 Portland food carts, 9 sailors surfing,
8 broncos bucking, 7 gray wolves howling, 6 boarders boosting,
5 snowy peaks, 4 thundereggs, 3 beavers,
2 waterfalls, and a meadowlark in a fir tree.

Oregon: The Beaver State

Capital: Salem · **State abbreviation:** OR · **Largest city:** Portland · **State bird:** the western meadowlark · **State flower:** the Oregon grape · **State tree:** the Douglas-fir · **State animal:** the American beaver · **State insect:** the Oregon swallowtail · **State rock:** the thunderegg · **State fish:** the Chinook salmon · **State crustacean:** the Dungeness crab · **State motto:** *Alis Volat Propiis* "She Flies With Her Own Wings" · **State song:** "Oregon, My Oregon" by J. A. Buchanan and Henry B. Murtagh

Some Famous Oregonians:

James Beard (1903–1985) was born in Portland. He grew up in a family that liked to cook and became a highly respected chef, teacher, writer, and television personality.

Beverly Cleary (1916–) is an award-winning children's book author. From an early age, she wanted to write funny stories about kids in her Northeast Portland neighborhood. Ramona Quimby, Henry Huggins, and a dog named Ribsy, all of Klickitat Street, are among the characters she created. Their sculptures can be seen in Portland's Grant Park, not far from the real Klickitat Street.

Abigail Scott Duniway (1834–1915) was born in Illinois and emigrated to Lafayette, Oregon, when she was seventeen. She was a writer, a journalist, a farmer, and a business owner, but was best known as an outspoken promoter of women's rights. She published a newspaper to spread her views, and spent 40 years working tirelessly to see that women were given the right to vote.

Matt Groening (1954–), born in Portland, is an artist and writer. He is the creator of *The Simpsons*, an Emmy award–winning television series featuring the daily ins and outs of a cartoon family.

Steve Prefontaine (1951–1975) was born in Coos Bay on the southern Oregon coast. He grew up to be a track star at the University of Oregon and held seven American records before his life was cut short in a car accident. His talent and dedication continue to inspire generations of runners, and his legacy has helped make Eugene the track and field capital of the world.

For the Grims with love, and many thanks to Robin Michal Koontz for her help and support. —S.B
For Suz, Meredith, Merideth, Jennifer, and Andrea. —C.C.

STERLING CHILDREN'S BOOKS
New York

An Imprint of Sterling Publishing
387 Park Avenue South
New York, NY 10016

STERLING CHILDREN'S BOOKS and the distinctive Sterling Children's Books logo are trademarks of Sterling Publishing Co., Inc.

Text © 2014 by Susan Blackaby
Illustrations © 2014 by Carolyn Conahan
The artwork for this book was created using watercolor paints on paper.
Designed by Andrea Miller and Jennifer Browning

ISBN 978-1-4549-0891-3

Library of Congress Cataloging-in-Publication Data

Blackaby, Susan, author.
  The Twelve days of Christmas in Oregon / by Susan Blackaby ; illustrated by Carolyn Conahan.
    pages cm
  Summary: Damon writes a letter home each of the twelve days he spends exploring the state of Oregon at Christmastime, as his cousin Liz and her family show him everything from the Columbia River Gorge to Portland, the "Rose City." Includes facts about Oregon.
  ISBN 978-1-4549-0891-3 (hardback)
  [1. Oregon--Fiction. 2. Christmas--Fiction. 3. Cousins--Fiction. 4. Letters--Fiction.] I. Conahan, Carolyn, illustrator. II. Title.

PZ7.B5318Twe 2014
[Fic]--dc23

2013047320

Distributed in Canada by Sterling Publishing
c/o Canadian Manda Group, 165 Dufferin Street
Toronto, Ontario, Canada M6K 3H6
Distributed in the United Kingdom by GMC Distribution Services
Castle Place, 166 High Street, Lewes, East Sussex, England BN7 1XU
Distributed in Australia by Capricorn Link (Australia) Pty. Ltd.
P.O. Box 704, Windsor, NSW 2756, Australia

For information about custom editions, special sales, and premium and corporate purchases, please contact
Sterling Special Sales at 800-805-5489 or specialsales@sterlingpublishing.com.

Manufactured in China
Lot #:
2 4 6 8 10 9 7 5 3 1
07/14

www.sterlingpublishing.com/kids

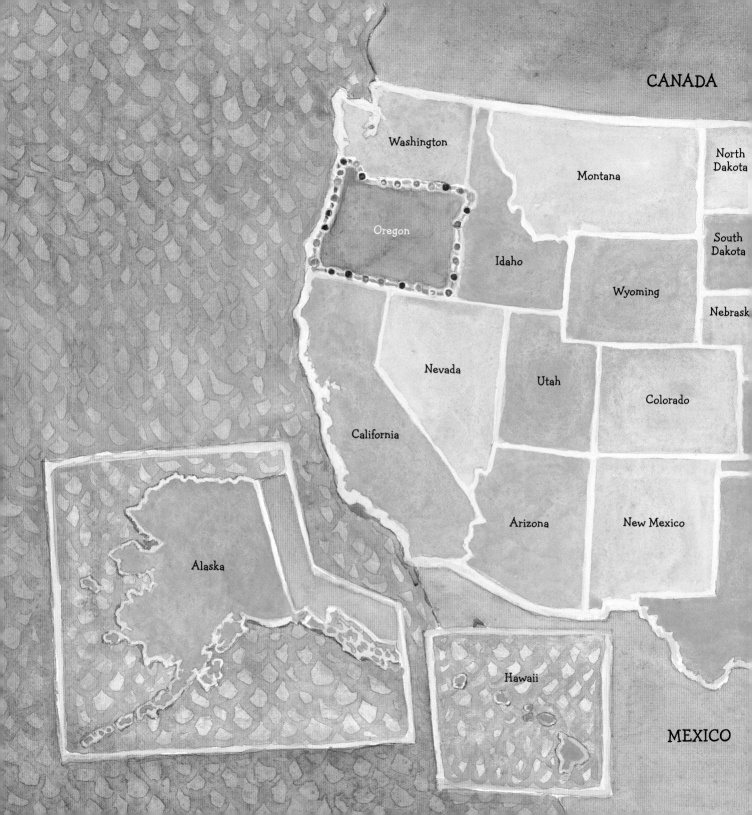

CANADA

Washington

Montana

North
Dakota

South
Dakota

Oregon

Idaho

Wyoming

Nebrask

Nevada

Utah

Colorado

California

Arizona

New Mexico

Alaska

Hawaii

MEXICO